TURBULENT

HYSTERICAL BOOKS

TURBULENT

Shane Allison

HYSTERICAL BOOKS
TALLAHASSEE, FL 2024

Turbulent by Shane Allison — First Edition

Cover Image: Shane Allison
Design, production: Jay Snodgrass

LOC: 2023948348
ISBN — 978-0-940821-22-4

Cover Image: Paren'ts Photo by Shane Allison

Hysterical Books is dedicated wholly
to the publication and appreciation
of fine poetry and other literary genres.

HYSTERICAL BOOKS
1506 Wekewa Nene
Tallahassee Florida

Published in the United States by Hysterical Books
Tallahassee, Florida • First Edition, 2023
hystericalbooks.com
hystericalbooks@gmail.com

For Betty & Frank

Contents

Greetings

Hey!

Hey, how are you?

Good. How are you?

Good. I'm good.

That's good, so what's up?

Nothing much. What's up with you?

Nothing much. So you're good?

Yeah, I'm doing good. I'm doing real good.

That's good.

Knock Out, Drag Out

As a kid I never liked boxing
But my dad could sit in the living room for hours,

Sucking marrow out of the bones of pork chops
And watch every round. I hated when he yelled and cursed

At the TV, spitting in the floor model faces of heavy weight champs.
How could he eat while men bounced around a ring with fat black eyes,

Noses that ran with blood, sweat trickling into cuts?
Slurp water from a plastic bottle, swish and spit.

Gloved fists, swollen faces.
Boxers got balls to take a ten round beat down.

Give me the Olympics, swimmers with swimmer builds,
German gymnasts gracefully somersaulting.

Give me water polo over knock out, drag out fights any day.
Dad watched until the last man was left standing

As I cringed to left hooks, right jabs,
Q-tips, laced with Vaseline used to seal busted lips.

TV Remote

There are too many buttons on this Trinitron remote.

I remember when life was so much simpler

Than muting.

The plus and negative of volumes and channels.

With the push of this I can destroy the world by simply pressing erase,

But I don't want that kind of domination.

I just need to know

Where the batteries go.

Black Kitchen

The bacon sizzles in a silver pot on a spiral top that burns
To a tangerine orange beneath sweet cabbage.

Turn that stove down low, boy!
Collard greens unfurl to the size of elephant ears.

Let the water run rinsing them clean.
Hand me the knife from the drawer.

Get the strainer ready for rice.
Here are the scissors to cut the chittlins'.

They don't smell as bad over rice,
Doused with hot sauce.

Seasoning salt is drizzled over
Honey-sweet ham.

It's 6p.m. Time to make the cornbread.
Mother makes the wild berry kool-aid syrupy sweet.

Slices of Aunt Earline's jelly cake

Lie like dominoes on a plate painted with porcelain roses.

Pork chops in a ceramic bowl

Sit sullenly next to store bought

Sweet potato pies.

I'm in my room writing poetry,

Waiting to sink my teeth into chicken breast

While the *Superfriends* are on mute.

Yall can come on eat now!

Frank

Frank, make sure you make a fire tonight

Don't leave your plate out on the table, Frank

Frank is never going to finish this house.

Frank, the boy don't do nothing but sit around the house.

Child, Frank is sorry.

Frank, are these your socks you left down here on the floor?

Clean out the tub, Frank

Frank back in jail again.

You better go tell Frank.

Did somebody call here for Frank?

Let's be frank

Is Frank there?

Beans & franks

Frankfurter

Frankenstein

Frankly my dear, I don't give a damn!

Father's Day

My daddy is the worse because he can't throw a ball very far. He also throws it too high.

My daddy doesn't help me with my homework, and he's not nice and I do not like him.

My daddy is not special because he is not very nice. The other thing I don't like about my daddy is that he doesn't play with me.

My daddy likes boating, but I don't like it. I do not like my daddy because he likes boating and I don't like it.

My daddy does not love me.

My daddy is not good because he does not take care of me.

My daddy does not take me fishing. He doesn't play sports with me. I do not love him.

I don't like my daddy because he doesn't take me places and is super mean to me.

My daddy is nothing like me. My daddy is never on TV.

My daddy doesn't play games on the computer with me.

My daddy is not funny.

My daddy is not great because he is not loving or caring. He doesn't make me feel happy.

My daddy is never there for me. He is the worse dad in the world.

My daddy doesn't play croquet with me in the back yard. He is not my best friend and I don't love him.

My daddy is not number one. Why? He doesn't support me, and he doesn't

love fishing.

My daddy hates fishing and I hate my daddy. He doesn't take time with me.

My daddy can't fix stuff for me. He never builds stuff for me.

My daddy doesn't work hard and always gives up. He doesn't like

to hunt a lot.

My daddy doesn't keep me safe.

My daddy never teaches me things.

My daddy can't pick me up and let me touch the ceiling. He can't pick up

my bike

And put me in his truck with me on the bike.

My daddy is the worse daddy in the whole wide world.

The idea of this poem was taken from a newspaper one year where, on Father's Day, children wrote in. Each one talked about how loving and special their fathers were. That was never the case with my own dad. Those sweet moments gave me the idea to write something on my dad that was anything but sweet.

Make Sure

Make sure you get these crumbs off the table.

Make sure you take out the trash.

Make sure you cut off the lights in the garage.

Cut the yard.

Did you see about getting some new glasses?

Don't forget to clean your room.

Make sure you buy the bus ticket and call Karen tomorrow.

Make sure you don't get any ink on the chair.

Make sure you pick up my business cards before the place closes.

Make sure you take down the Christmas decorations.

You've gained so much weight.

You need to drink plenty of water.

Call me when you get back to New York.

Make sure you see your grandma before you leave,

Here, mail the *DirectTV* bill.

I thought I told you to move those boxes out of the garage.

Make sure you're home by 5 o. clock. I want to go to a program.

Make sure you get something to eat.

I'm not cooking.

The Week before My Mother Goes
to Have Her Bunions Removed

I'm going into surgery next week, she says.

I'm going to need you to help me out for a few days.

I'm finally going to have these bunions removed,

So you and your daddy need to keep the house clean.

I'm going to need you to help me out for a few days.

These things know they hurt.

Make sure you and your daddy keep the house clean.

I'll be able to wear heels again.

These things know they hurt.

The doctor said he has to cut the bone and realign the joints.

I'll be able to wear descent shoes again.

Are you scared? I asked.

The doctor said he has to cut the bone and realign the joints.

No, I'm not scared. I just want to get it over with.

Are you sure you're not scared?

A little bit.

I just want to get it over with.

The doctor said he's going to have to do the right foot first.

I'm scared,

But I don't have to wear a cast or anything.

The doctor said he's going to work on the right foot first,

And I got to stay off of it for six weeks,

But I don't have to wear a cast or anything.

I might need you to help me to the bathroom.

I got to stay off the foot for six weeks

Or it'll start throbbing,

So I might need you to help me to the bathroom.

I'll take care of you, I told her.

Lotion

Not sure how much more is left

So I press the hole to my eye.

Hammer the bottle into my palm for any signs.

A light scent, non-greasy formula.

The size of a dime passed around fingers,

Smeared inside the dips of elbows,

Behind that place where the knees bend,

Between the spaces of toes.

Rub it over round curves of shoulders,

Across the faint scar on my thigh from the crock pot burn.

Grandmother's Pocket Book

Grandma, what's in your pocket book?

You got any drink coasters in your pocket book?

You got any porcelain Siamese cats in your pocket book, grandma,

Or stale barbecue potato chips at the bottom of your pocket book?

Grandma, do you have a Teflon frying pan in your pocket book?

Do you have a nutcracker, or small bottles of whiskey in your pocket book,

The ones you find in hotel room refrigerators?

What about a pair of earrings?

Do you have any sterling silver earrings in your pocket book, grandma?

What about a cashmere sweater or a pair of flannel boxers?

Grandma, what about a couple of golf balls? Got any in your pocket book?

Do you have any wire frogs or turtles made from wire in your pocket book?

Grandma, how about some peach blossom air freshener? Do you have a

can in your pocket book?

Grandma, what about remote control cars with remote controls.

Do you have any of those in your pocket book?

Do you have a pair of raspberry-colored Barbie boots in your pocket book?

Do you have a French poodle in your pocketbook or a pair of jelly sandals

in teal?

How about a pair of pink jeans, or a tie-dyed muscle t-shirt?

Any unicorns in that pocket book of yours, grandma?

How about some fairy dust?

Grandma, can I have a calculator watch and some crazy glue

If you have those things in your pocketbook?

You wouldn't by any chance have a boyfriend with a bubble bear-butt

In your pocket book for me would you?

Do you have a orange windbreaker in your pocket book for me? It's a little

chilly.

Do you have a slaw dog and a strawberry-banana slushy in your pocket

book?

I skipped lunch.

Grandma, do you have a pair of fat rat shoestrings in your pocketbook

I could use to lace up my Adidas'

Grandma, I lost a sling shot with a white handle.

I've looked everywhere for it. Can I check your pocket book?

Do you have a polka-dot turtleneck in your pocket book or some clip-n-

save coupons?

Grandma, let me get a honey bun and a dime bag of coke if you got it on

hand In your pocket book.

Thank you, grandma. I owe ya one.

Innocence Lost

The slurs of his words sliced through the crowd of school bus kids.

Hey faggot!

Didn't know he meant me until I heard my name.

In grade school he was a pop rock,

The kind of firecracker -crazy no teacher could control.

The only Indian boy at Woodville Elementary.

His parents didn't live far from the school.

We were friends horse-playing like wild mustangs,

Relay racing down monkey bars.

I would exchange my Apple sauce for his fruit roll-up.

We lost our innocence in junior high cliques

When sides had to be picked.

I lost Sammie when I came out to him between shelves of library books.

No way, no way! He kept saying, as if I told him I was carrying cooties.

I didn't see him until three years later

Where he was older, looking more like his mother.

Thinking back on it, I should have broken him in several places,

Should have raided his back pack for chocolate pudding cups,

Should have eaten his skin like a fruit roll-up.

Department Store

All bed pillows

All beach towels

All down comforters

All wall décor frame framed wall art and mirrors

All frames, albums and scrapbook kits

All custom decorating galaxy collection fabrics

All bath rugs

All solid color towels

All sheets and sheet sets

All blankets and throws

All bed-in-a-bag comforter sets, bedspreads and quilts

All juvenile bedding and accessories

All mattress pads

All games and clocks

All mattress and metal pads

All wicker bath accents

All accent and area rugs

All decorative pillows

All table linens

All decorative accessories and replacement shades

All pet gifts

All bath accessories

All shower curtains

All bath scales

All Comfort Zone therapeutic pillows

All Comfort Zone therapeutic mattress pads

All bedroom furniture

All dining rooms plus two free chairs w/ a 5-pc set purchase

All home office and entertainment centers

All sectionals, sofas and recliners

All occasional tables

All accent furniture and curios

All furniture accessories

All ready-made window coverings

All home collection candles

Are 30 percent off of regular price

When I Tell You

When I tell you I saw my father's dick by mistake when I was eleven,

You say, *I don't want that image in my head.*

You don't want to hear that he gets 5k a month from the VA for his service

in Vietnam?

I don't think he ever picked up a gun,

Never eased a finger off a trigger

That wasn't his own dick.

It's the only thing I wish I had inherited from him

Instead of his lying eyes and slick mouth,

That Melvin Street nose he blows due to hay fever.

You don't want to know how we pass each other

In the house like two ships at sea?

You should see the looks he gives me.

Had I been born straight,

Had I turned out like my sister

Armed with a husband and three children,

His love would have been better

No, you don't want to hear

About the jelly jar of tears my mother has spilled,

The hate that stirs in me.

Drama Queen

After Vytautas Pliura's poem, "My Mother is Jean Harlow"

Your mama might be Jean Harlow but my mama is Joan Crawford.

She never beat me with wire hangers, but she tore my ass up with

Leather belts and bedroom shoes.

Instead of scrubbing the bathroom floor with Dutchman cleanser,

I had to clean out the garage and mow the yard.

I helped her to the toilet after she went to the

Doctor to have her bunions removed.

She never fed me milk and cookies after school,

Didn't bake cakes or knit sweaters.

My mama was never into PTA meetings or dinner parties.

She delivered telephone books door to door.

She never came to see me play Santa Claus in my third grade Christmas play.

My mama is Cleopatra Jones with AK-47's

And grenades in the glove box of her Monte Carlo.

So what if your mama is a Blonde Bombshell,

Mine hot curls her hair, greases it with hair mayonnaise.

So what if you grew up on a farm churning buttermilk, stepping in Angus shit?

I went to a high school where the principal said

I exposed my dick to some supposed white girl.

Her name was privileged information.

Who cares if your mother is Jean Harlow

My mama is Wonder Woman catching missiles like Frisbees,

Bending crowbars with dishpan hands.

She's a housekeeper emptying garbage cans of hazardous waste,

Bringing home smothered chicken on Styrofoam plates.

Does Jean Harlow know how to cook neck bones and rice

I bet she doesn't know how to make Jiffy mix cornbread?

So what if she's Jean Harlow?

If she's so famous then she won't mind if we invite a few friends

Over to her place for a pool party,

Watch her old movies that made her a star.

Do you think old Jean can lend me a couple of bucks

To pay back my student loans?

Haiku

Dennis the Menace

Nothing to do but write poems

Sweat pours down my balls

Spaghetti

For years she couldn't get it right,

Pouring cords of pasta into a pot of water.

At one point out of desperation,

She would add spoons of butter

Because everyone knows butter

 Makes everything delicious.

My sister and I would get plates of gummy, chewy spaghetti

While our father has never been a fan.

He grew up on souse and stewed turtle,

Tripe and pig feet.

He would help himself to a plate, but had no appetite for much.

I always know what's for dinner after seeing

Two packs of ground beef thawing in the sink.

My mother finally got it right

When Sheryl, her best friend told her she had to wait for the water

To get hot before pouring the noodles.

I eat more of the meat trying to separate myself from the carbs.

It's better a few days later when I add hot sauce,

Diced garlic instead of onions.

From what I've googled, the sauce is homemade

Not House style out of a jar.

The meatballs are the size of fists.

I miss Michael's version that included slices of sausage with olive oil.

That reminds me.

I need to DM him to get the recipe.

Neck-Deep

There's no hiding behind walls,

No crawling on your hands and knees,

Ducking flashlights,

Peering through sliding glass doors.

You can't hold sheriffs back behind padlocked fences,

Their guns loaded and cocked.

They twirl handcuffs around their fingers like hula-hoops,

Waving night sticks.

It's only a matter of time.

I'm going to get him one way or the other

If I have to hunt him down, the U.S. Marshal said.

You'll be in a jail cell by the end of the week,

Eating jail-issued dinners,

Wearing a navy jumpsuit, those ugly white plastic sandals.

You're going to be a seven-numbered prison bitch.

I would rather die than go to jail, you said,

As you cried in the living room.

Mama will wait by the phone for your collect calls

To hear your empty promises.

Lord, how are we gonna pay these bills, she said.

As she paces the kitchen floor,

Snot trickling out of her nose,

Her eyes red and puffy.

Hiding is futile.

They have four warrants out on you.

I'm done lying, through denying.

They're going to bust up this family,

Wake the whole neighborhood

With sirens of emergency.

They're going to put you under the jail this time.

I just know it.

Darrin

Karen swore she saw you at a crack house on Melvin Street.

No one can explain how you have lost all that weight.

It turned out to be diabetes.

Let me just say that I never thought you were on drugs.

No one knows how you lost all that weight.

You used to look like the rapper Ice-Cube.

Karen swore she saw you at a crack house on Melvin Street.

As kids, we never got along.

You used to look like the rapper Ice-Cube.

We fought all the time.

As kids we never got along.

You always won the fights for being bigger and older than me.

We fought all the time.

I hated it when you used to pick on me.

You always won the fights for being bigger and older than me.

Always getting into trouble at school.

I hated you picking on me.

You dropped out after being accused of having drugs in your locker

After getting into trouble at school.

Now you're a garbage collector.

You dropped out after being accused of having drugs in your locker.

I feel so sorry for you, Darrin

Being a garbage collector and all.

I never thought you would stoop so low.

I feel so sorry for you, Darrin.

You need to get off your ass.

I never thought you would stoop so low.

You need to stop feeling sorry for yourself.

Garage Sale

Do you have any poems written on the walls in your house?

Do you have a pair of Reebok sneakers

in your house or one of those artificial

plants? Do you have a Sony TV on a scratched

coffee table in your house? What about one of those

exercise bikes? Do you have any shadeless lamps

in your house or old kerosene lamps

from back in the day? Do you have in your house,

bumper-stickers on the walls? Do you have one of those

plug-in air-fresheners? Do you have a pair of dirty sneakers

lying around the house? Do you have a sofa all scratched

up by your house cat? Do you have any artificial

flowers in your house, or a set of artificial

limbs collecting dust someplace? I could use a few crystal lamps.

Is there a room being remodeled in your house? Got any scratched

up records from the seventies in your house?

I need two two-by fours and a pair of sneakers

with fat rat shoe laces. Do you have one of those

digital clocks or one of those

water beds with bed rails with artificial

wheels on them? Do you have a set of sneakers

sitting in a rocking chair in your house? Got any old lamps

in the attic of your house,

or a few pieces of scratched

up dinnerware in your house that's been scratched

up? Do you have a few of those

plum-purple pillows in your house

somewhere? What I really need is an artificial

stuffed deer head. Do you have any lava lamps

that you don't want or some old sneakers

chewed up by some old dog who likes to chew old sneakers

that you don't want anymore? I'm looking for a brown scratched

up suitcase. I could use a laundry basket filled with Genie lamps.

Do you have one of those

electric blankets in your house, or an artificial

gold elephant charm lying about in your house?

Do you have any of those scratched up

artificial teki lamps lying around in your house?

I'll give you the sneakers off my feet for one.

Spit & Vinegar & Fried Pork Chops

I can smell them at the door.

The aroma keeps the hound dogs behind the house howling.

The scent of spices and seasonings mixes

In the wet air after a hard rain.

The last thing I had on my stomach

Was birthday cake popcorn

From a Barnes & Noble Café.

The den is done from the remodeling,

African decor align the walls.

The picture of my grandparents brings it all together.

I have sired it *The Mirror Room.*

My father has been home most of the day

Flipping channels, never settling on anything for too long.

I sit the bills from TJmaxx, Bealls and Home Depot

Behind a picture of me at seventeen

Wearing a rayon shirt, my face peppered with blackheads.

I rests my back pack against a bin filled with portfolios of art.

The smell of grease is thick in the kitchen.

Corn on the cob soaks in a pot of buttered water.

The peas are cooked from a can.

The heap of white rice raises the A1C,

So I make a sandwich instead.

I take Rosuvastatin for the cholesterol.

Must lose twenty pounds to be eligible for my knee surgery.

Mother has been held up in her room all week

Only coming out to clean, cook and do a few loads of laundry.

I assume she's still pissed with my father

About letting Pee-Wee in the house to

Help move the tables into the mirror room.

Just when I'm about to take my plate into the kitchen,

I'm an eye witness to her banging on my father's bedroom door.

She's full of spit & vinegar

Because the breaker keeps tripping,

Interrupting an episode of *Gun Smoke*.

When she turns to face me,

I shut the door to her heat,

To keep from getting burned.

Racoon

Go fetch Pee-Wee, the crack head from next door.

He'll do anything for a buck.

With a nickname like that, maybe even suck your dick.

An act I wouldn't want to see performed

On my own father.

Grab the tallest ladder and set it at the start of the attic

Where you store the old Christmas tree,

And boxes of decorations you don't need anymore,

Because this is a house

Where things are not celebrated,

Where you can't remember the last bright toy that

Was pushed along these cold floors.

I would do it but I'm afraid of heights

And feral creatures with teeth for biting hands.

You are as rickety as the ladder

With your two bad knees and in no shape to fight a raccoon.

Come in the room, stand here,

Directly over these panels of silver.

You can hear it scrounging and scratching about

Trying to find a way out.

Who knows how long it's been up there

Without food, lusting for freedom.

Labor Room One

I saw the video about the first trimester

Sitting on top of the VCR.

This was different than snitching on you

For spilling Kool aid on the floor,

For not cleaning out the bathtub.

When the news broke,

It spread across the family like a fever.

I thought our father was going to lock you away

Someplace, cut off from all light.

Instead, he didn't speak to you for days

Thinking he had lost his little girl.

Mother looked to me as if I had a backpack full of answers.

She shared her fears over grape soda & spiced ham sandwiches.

The Kleenex from crying

Was strewn across rose- pink carpet.

Karen in Queens was the first to be told.

The aunt everyone likes.

I watched your belly balloon

Under MC Hammer and Al B. Sure t-shirts,

Walking the halls of the house with shame in your face.

To think… you would be crowned mother in a matter of months.

Me, an uncle to your first born.

Our father sat in his dark of disappointment

As mother held your hand through contractions,

I sat outside labor room one.

I sat outside fisting the cushions

Of the chair beneath me.

Hearing your sighs,

Your cries from behind the door.

Teddy stood over you

Waiting for fatherhood.

I didn't think much of the man

Who knocked up my sister

I used to watch cartoons with,

I used to trade rap tapes with.

Hours later my niece slipped out into this world,

Her face full of life.

When we got home with our crowns,

Mother entered the house with rage

For a husband too angry to hold his granddaughter

She kicked his bedroom door open

Where our father was sleeping to have her say.

I went to bed, happy about the new edition to the family.

Looking for Jasmin

Mama woke me up

Screaming like she was crazy.

I can't find her, I can't find Jaz! Have you seen her?

She searched every room,

Stomping through the den,

The blue and white kitchen,

The dining room with beige, stained carpet.

My niece is lost, a grandmother frantic in the house.

I wipe sleep out of my eyes, stung by the sun.

I check outside in the driveway, the garage,

Behind plastic bags of winter clothes.

I found her, Mama yelled.

Where was she?

She was in my bathroom

About to flush my dentures down the toilet.

My Niece Refuses to Get Behind the Wheel
of Her Pink Barbie Car

My niece won't go near her pink 4x4 Barbie jeep.

For months it's all she yelled about. *I want Barbie car, I want Barbie car.*

My mother and father went to every store in town to find it:

Target, Toys-R-Us, but no luck until they went to a Wal-Mart

In Tifton Georgia. They bought the last one they had in stock.

Father spent hours in the den putting it together.

Connecting the purple, plastic power wheels,

Inserting this bit and that piece into slot A, slot B.

Sweat dripped into the crease of the paper

As he tried to read the directions without his glasses.

According to the speedometer on the sticker, it can go 120 miles per hour.

Christmas morning we all watched her climb

Into the driver's seat of her pink Barbie car.

She turned the fake radio knobs for some cruising tunes.

When she pressed her little foot against the plastic,

White peddle to make it go,

She ran it into in-tables, newly painted walls.

My mother laughed; my niece started crying.

She wasn't ready for such independence.

We offered to take it outside

But she refused to go near it even with her doll, Wendy-Walk- With- Me

Accompanying her in the passenger seat.

Now it sits in the garage. The pink seatbelts collecting dust.

All that power steering gone to waste.

But she's not afraid of her white, blue, and yellow bicycle

With the training wheels and no brakes.

The bike she rides on down the living room hallway

Across a newly mopped kitchen floor,

Running over my foot in the process.

Aunt Karen Sestina

Dear Karen, I am sick as a dog.

Been coughing and sneezing all weekend

And the thing is, it's not that cold

Down here in Tallahassee. But that's what I get

For going out without my jacket on at night.
I left all of my good coats at your house,

So now I don't have a single coat in the house

To put on for this kind of weather. My neighbor's dog

Is healthier than me. You should hear me coughing at night.

Ma makes fun of me when I cough. I spent the whole weekend

In bed. I went to the drugstore to get
Some Alka-Seltzer Plus. It's the cold

And flu kind. I can't stand having a cold.

I think my coats and sweaters are in a suitcase at your house.

Would you be a dear and get

Them out of the suitcases? They must smell like wet dog

By now. I might go see the new Harry Potter movie this weekend.
Is Tarisha still into it? Ma told me last night

That ya'll lost twenty pounds. All I do is snack all night,

But I haven't had much of an appetite with this cold.

I've been drinking lots of juice. I think last weekend

Was when I caught it, when I left the house

Without a jacket. I wish I had a dog
To keep me company. I'm gonna get

Me one once I'm out on my own. I'm gonna get

A few cats and hamsters, too. They're good at night

When you need them to fetch something. The neighbor's dog

Is gorgeous. I heard on the news that it's inhumane to leave animals

out in the cold.

So has Will done any work to the house?
I miss coming over to see you on the weekends.

Do you and Tarisha still go to Long Island on the weekends?

Before you come home for Christmas, can you run by and get

Me a crack head lunch with an extra bag of chips? In your house

I like the lavender and yellow room downstairs. I called you last night,

But you weren't home. I need to get rid of this cold.
I am sicker than a crack head lunch-eating crack head. Dog,

It's cold in New York. Is the house still

Warm upstairs and cold downstairs?

You better get yourself a dog to keep you warm at night.

Haiku

I'm missing my shows

Roof leaks rain water

Gas lamp lights my way

For My Mother Who Asks, "Why is Your Stomach so Big?"

My belly is my hurt locker

Where I hold years of pain,

And the kind of anger that destroys

Towns like a Tennessee tornado and there are no survivors.

No matter how many pushups I do,

I will never burn off this bitterness.

Every stretch mark is a daisy chain of memories.

This one tells the story of the day dad beat me

Because I embarrassed him

In front of his former high school football coach

For not dressing out in gym.

This one tells of the day he went to prison for a year

And we had to rustle up dinner by standing in line at food banks.

This one that trails down to my thigh

Tells of the look you gave me

When that mall cop told you

I was being arrested for indecent exposure.

These stretch marks mark the night

You told me you would rather be dead

Than have a gay son. Do you remember?

I was only nineteen and not as sweet.

This one that leads down to my belly button

Is the day dad called me a sissy.

I heard him outside the bathroom window.

So in case you're wondering what happened to me,

Why I won't be the son you want me to be,

It's not due to fried chicken or pork chop sandwiches,

Or late night snacks of raisin cream pies

Or nutty buddies,

But a rage unlike anything you will ever know, Mother.

American Father

My old man was a strict old man.

My old man kept a tight leash around my sister.

My old man said, *she's not coming in this house at all times of the night.*

My old man made her cry when he beat her with a switch.

My old man cheated on my mother while I was in her belly.

My old man was a high school quarterback.

   I remember when my old man would take me to Lee's barbershop to get a
haircut.

My old man was a liar and a cheat.

My old man only likes vanilla flavored ice cream.

My old man prefers small towns to big cities.

My old man might know a lot about fixing things, but ask him

    To bring up the internet on his phone, and he's lost.

My old man leaves dirty socks and underwear on the coffee table before
bed.

My old man went to jail for a year leaving us to fend for ourselves with no
money.

My old man crawled on his hands and knees on the living room floor

    When the sheriffs shined a flashlight through the windows.

    I have never seen my old man in handcuffs.

My old man faked a heart attack in jail.

My old cried when his mama died.

My old man served in Vietnam, and got a hunting knife for his tour of duty.

He let it rust in the rain.

I watched my old man try to beat my mama once, but she wasn't having it.

My old man called me a sissy.

My old man taught me how to drive when I was fourteen.

My old man had a Volkswagen he called, "Blue Magic." He let it rust in the backyard.

My old man stole packs of meat and chicken out of Winn-Dixie.

One of my old man's brothers, they call "The Chicken Man," eats raccoons and squirrels.

My old man eats souse, hog head cheese and pig feet.

My old man's old high school football buddies was always asking me when I was going to try out for football.

My old man has the worst bad breath.

My old man has all this dirt under his fingernails.

My old man fell out of a tree once and broke his shoulder.

My old man puts too much milk in his cereal.

My old man with his nappy beard and fungal toenails.

My old man yells and curses when his favorite college football team is losing.

My old man has the worst case of hey favor.

My old man watches porn when he thinks everyone's asleep.

My old man stinks up the bathroom.

My old man violated his probation.

My old man likes hot sauce on everything.

My old man leaves a fuck-ton of dirt in the bathtub.

My old man's best friend, Bruce, died from a heart attack while mowing his yard.

 My old man's tank tops and old football jockstrap from high school.

My old man leaves piss on the toilet.

My old man loves my Aunt Earline's coconut cake.

My old man is like a lot of old men.

I hate my old man.

I love my old man.

Dreams & Nightmares

I once had a nightmare

That my father was a monster

With glowing red eyes.

My mother has been mauled

By him many times,

Chewed up until only bones remained.

Still, she remains.

I had a dream you died,

Measured for a military uniform

For a military funeral

Where men from the Waffle House

Wait in line to thank you for your service.

If only they knew of the atrocities

You have committed.

Belt

I threw it away yesterday in a waste basket

Of orange peels,

Junk mail,

Scraps from collages,

And empty vitamin water bottles.

Something came loose from the buckle

That I tossed in the bathroom trashcan

Between the toilet and shower curtain.

It wasn't the same belt my father used to beat me,

Or the belt I thought to hang myself with in the garage.

This is the one worn away at the punch holes

Purchased from Wal-Mart for twelve bucks

With leather strong enough to hold me together.

Oh, to be replaced like an old sock,

Or a pair of underwear with a shotty waistband.

Lamps

I'm in my bedroom eating chicken wings and salad

For dinner when my mother walks in asking if I have seen her lamps.

What lamps? I ask.

The credits from *Law & Order: SVU* reflect in the lens of my Armani

eyeglasses.

The ones like in my room with the silver base, she says.

She has taken over the house with tote bags of shoes,

Bumblebee bins stacked by threes.

A tattered comforter covers a rack of well outdated coats and jackets.

One night my father called to me to help my mother out of a hoard

She had built by her own hand,

Fussing to rescue blouses, suits, and skirts

From a leaky roof as if her clothes were her children

She was fighting to save out of a fire.

An assortment of hats hang on a coat rack

In front of my sister's old room.

Necklaces, earrings and bracelets scattered across her dresser.

Last week she was in an uproar about

A picture of my grandmother and grandfather she couldn't find.

I found it hidden behind a treasure chest of bed sheets.

My father must have saved it from plumes of dust and debris

The handymen were kicking up

While uprooting base board and rotted floor.

Those lamps didn't get up and walk away from here, she says.

I know what she's thinking; the accusation that's running through her head.

My father and I pay her no mind as she searches

Among stacks of kitchen mats, rugs and ice-cream laundry baskets.

I return to my dinner with Captain Benson where the chicken wings are

Cold and the lettuce lies limp in peppercorn dressing.

An hour later in the garage, my mother finds the lamps in a corner

Next to the bumblebee storage bins

That are stacked way too high for her to reach.

Husband and Wife

She's been quiet all week.

I walked past her as she was gathering dishes to wash,

Sectioning last night's dinner to be stored

In the fridge, and she acted as if I wasn't there.

I don't care.

I've got my own crosses to bear.

I'm sure she's upset with my father again about something he did or didn't do,

Didn't take the trash to the dump,

Stained the sheets with blood from his insulin needle,

Withdrew money out of the bank without telling her again.

No one knows.

I can always tell when something's wrong.

A darkness comes over the house

As if there's been a death.

The tension is like a choking smoke.

No one holds a grudge like my mother.

Spite runs hot in her blood. It simmers, but never cools.

She's got everyone fooled but me.

My sister talks to her with sugar in her voice.

Once my father is done in from the electro shocks of her silent treatment,

He'll corner her with a mouthful of apologies

Never knowing what he's sorry for.

Anything to get back in her good graces

Until the next fight.

Brass Knuckles

I have a job for you.
I want you to bitch-slap my father with a hand armed with a set
                              of brass knuckles.
Every time he cuts me with one of those looks like he's afraid
                         of having a faggot for a son,
Belt him in the guts until he buckles over and throws up the bacon & eggs
He ate at the Waffle House.
I can pay you plenty if that's what worries you.

My father gets five grand a month for his service in Vietnam.
I doubt the old bastard has ever shot a gun.
Ron Desantis says I don't need a permit,
Even if I'm crazier than a sack of cats.
I would love to see the look on my father's face when I point it at him
At the dinner table.

Every time my father lies, I want you to southpaw his ass in the jaw.
I want to hear the sound his bones make when they break.
Now before you say no, I want you to sleep on it.
Pray about it if you're a boy of the old book.
Name your price.
Call me if you'll take the job.

Shortness of Breath

After two months it finally broke.

With three prescriptions and an inhaler,

One would hope so.

Every bookstore and mall shopper looked at me

As if I was coughing right in their faces,

Directly down their throats.

I've tried everything: *Robitussin, Nyquil,* even *Mucinex*

Which is no good for my blood sugar,

But is the best stuff on the market

According to the hot CVS pharmacist who drives the F350 out front.

I thought turmeric tea would burn it out,

I thought microwaved water with a lemon slice accent

Would chase it off.

I even tried warm milk.

All of them seem to act like temporary bandages

On an already infected wound.

Last night and many nights before,

I've had to pry myself up in bed,

Lie my head on several pillows stolen from my mother.

Someone finally said something.

My father.

You need to do something about that coughing.

He was right, so I did.

I took the last of the doxycycline yesterday

That insisted I remain upright for an hour.

Took the only prednisone left this morning.

To think there were sixty of those dolls when I started.

Bye-bye benzos

I'm convinced something evil has taken hold.

The Albuterol is all I have left in the form of an inhaler.

It's back to turmeric tea,

Hot water with lemon,

Cocoa in my *Doctor Who* mug.

Alone

They left this morning for my nephew's high school graduation in Orlando,

So I have the place to myself to do with what I want.

Maybe I'll invite a few guys over, maybe smoke some weed, or throw a

house party.

Nah, I don't have enough friends to fill a bathroom,

And I'm too old for drunken tomfoolery.

I'll probably just make art, write, and walk around naked,

Jack off to *Pornhub* or to Instagram pics some Instagram friends sent.

My niece, Jasmin, the girl born in labor room one,

Graduated from college last week.

I wasn't invited because she could only get four tickets,

Yet my parents were able to attend.

Guess the brats are waiting on money and gift cards

From the uncle they never call.

Jasmin looks more and more like her mother.

Probably got ways like her too. Snooty and bougie.

The last picture I saw of TJ he had his dad's nose

And was on the football team.

No one talks about him being any good.

They never ask about me,

And I don't have their numbers to call and ask about them.

This is a terrible excuse but I've never been much for family.

Probably because hugs and love were never given out at my house.

Let my parents tell it, and we're the god-damned Huxtable's.

My sister and I were close like any siblings.

Fought over the front seat,

Danced to *MC Hammer, Salt n Pepa*, the overweight lover himself, *Heavy*

D and The Boys.

When I told my sister it feels like we're ten thousand miles apart

She responded by saying,

That's because when I moved away, we went in separate directions

As if that's some kind of excuse not to phone to ask how your only brother

Is doing instead of getting second hand info from our mother.

It's whatever.

Uncles don't mean much,

Don't come with the kind of value a parent or grandparent holds.

I'm a poet so that must make me weird.

I'm queer, so I'm never to be loved,

And my name is not to be spoken at family dinners.

I can't make the trip to this graduation either.

I have a date with an ortho nurse to get cortisone

Injected in my knee.

Parents probably bickered all the way down there anyway.

This house is mine for the day

With its fridge full of food,

Its rooms full of quiet

To do what I want in as long as I clean up the mess before morning.

Haiku

Hurricane Dennis

Compose poems under white light

Broken power line

The Cough

Hell if I know where it came from.

Maybe I caught it at work,

Or hanging out at the bars too much.

Something has come over me,

Has taken a hold and won't let up.

Now here I am popping prednisone

Before my morning piss, benzos

Every eight hours,

Washing down horse size doxycycline

With full glasses of water

When the only results I seem to be getting are trips to the bathroom.

I blow into an inhaler for the wheezing

That feels like the devil is whistling Dixie

In my chest. I tell them everything about me

At the urgent care clinic, checking the only two boxes

That pertain to my health. Amlodipine for the hypertension,

Metformin for the borderline diabetes.

Bad blood runs in my family. The nurse pokes and prods

My nose to test me for Covid-19.

The doctor steps in armed in blue, wearing a face shield.

He greets me with a latex gloved knuckle bump.

A series of questions roll off his tongue.

A set of answers push past my lips into unsterile air.

He presses the bell of the stethoscope

At different points in my back as I take deep, labored breaths.

He moves around the front of my chest

Checking for any signs of crackling.

I hope he can do something. I pray he's the angel

That can kill this devil.

I prepare myself for any blood they may need.

I feel much better than I did Saturday night,

Coughing uncontrollably into my comforter.

Not even the thought of blue eyes could lull me to sleep.

Perhaps this is my punishment for the company I keep,

for all the whisky I drink,

For not introducing enough vitamin-c

Into my diet of fried and fast food.

Has a curse been put on my name?

Who walks around with a doll in my likeness,

Sticking pins in, pulling at the seams of this body?

Sick Inside

Word has it that Rebecca has it.

Has quarantined herself in that ratty apartment.

Probably caught it from one of her gentleman friends,

Or picked it up in Europe kissing on some Parisian boy.

Everyone knows her vagina is a revolving door.

Chris has come down with something, but no one is saying what exactly.

Savannah tested positive last year, but is negative this year.

I'm not surprised Kodi has it. He should stay away from people even if he

doesn't have it.

My dad has to lock himself away from the civilized for fourteen days.

He can't stay out of people's face.

Dominic and Ian swear they don't have it.

How can anyone be sure? I want to see their vax cards.

Mike called out sick again.

Kyle's been coughing but no cough out of the ordinary.

Has Jacob been tested?

Has that new girl Cheryl been vaccinated?

Carl's results came back.

John says he's getting tested tomorrow.

Has anyone seen Nate?

Scott's been complaining about shortness of breath.

Lawrence doesn't believe in it for watching too much Fox news.

What's the latest death toll?

If you don't like wearing a mask,

You will hate wearing a respirator. I read that on a poster at the clinic.

This feels like that movie *Outbreak*

Where Dustin Hoffman and Rene Russo

Race around in haz mat suits to find a monkey

That looks like a childhood toy I use to have.

Kevin Spacey's character died in that movie.

My mother told me they had Toad's funeral last weekend.

Bet he caught it from those crack heads he sold crack to.

I haven't been able to smell or taste anything for two weeks.

But let's keep that between us, okay?

Hell to Pay

Are you ready

Brace yourself

They're coming

Cops

Are you up

Hold on

Sirens

The boys in blue have a warrant for you

The day is coming

Brace yourself

Are you ready

Hold on tight

Prepare for the worst

Liar

You can't hide

You'll get more than eight months this time

They're coming for you

They're coming

Brace yourself

You stole

You cheated

Such a disappointment

Get the bail money ready

Are you ready

Men with guns

You can't hide

I won't lie for you

They're gonna put you under the jail this time

Hold on

Prepare for the worst

Bracing ourselves

Handcuffs

The sirens wake the neighbors

You're such a disappointment

You'll be in jail by this time next week, Daddy.

Get ready

Brace yourself

They're coming for you

Trading Places

The worry was starting to grow like an unwanted ear hair.

I was going to ask the new girl in the Doc Martens and pig tails

What happened, if you were alright,

But figured you were on vacation someplace,

Maybe on a Bible retreat with your church.

Your presence is a favorite blanket around me,

A jacket I wear with everything, not caring if it matches.

My father is not as soft-spoken as you.

He lives hard, eating bags of pork skins

Drowned in hot sauce until he passes out

On the bathroom floor, face down in the blood from his upper GI tract.

They found four polyps up his ass

That could have easily led to prostate cancer.

Speaking of which, how is your prostate?

Have you ever been in prison?

My father has.

It was a year of the best kind of peace

Without being bothered by worry.

Do you know what it's like to be wrestled

To the ground in your underwear by U.S Marshall's?

Tangerine orange and jelly sandals suits my father.

Do you know he keeps secrets like piggy bank pennies?

That he rattles my mother like a snack machine?

Had she met and married you,

I would have Spanish blood in these veins.

I don't think you could take my mother.

She doesn't bite her tongue about anything

If she doesn't approve of something.

My dad has threatened to leave several times,

Has shown signs of suicide.

He don't have no get up and go about his self

Is something she loves to say about my father.

He's not church-going like you. None of us are 'cept for funerals.

I prefer weddings over funerals.

When I recommended that my mother divorce my father

In the same courthouse they exchanged vows

In she said, *I'm not doing that. It would kill him.*

What she really meant was that it would kill her.

If my father were to kick it,

I have no doubt, she would jump into the casket

Screaming and crying hysterically,

Embarrassing us all.

How about you come over for dinner.

Mother makes the best baked chicken and yellow rice.

We can sit, pray and eat.

You can talk to my parents about adopting me as your own

Even if I am fifty and past my prime.

It's never too late to get a dad I can be proud of,

Who isn't slick with lies in his eyes,

Who doesn't look at me like a mistake he made.

So how about it?

Here's my number.

Call me soon with your answer.

Starter Kit Drag Queen

Sassy left one of her dresses in my car again.

Always happens when she's had too many vodka red bulls.

Carl cut her off,

Told the bartenders she isn't to be served alcohol

Until she's done hosting the show.

Sassy stumbles and slurs her words on stage.

When I notice make-up smudges on my upholstery,

Sequins in the passenger seat, who else could it be?

I take her dress, her wigs and gaudy fake jewelry

From the backseat, and slip it into the house,

Lie it all on the bed like a piece of trade I've picked up from the bar.

I take a few drinks from leftover bottled water

To flush out the shots and well booze.

I'm not as drunk as Sassy tonight.

I hold up the cotton polyester blend

With its yellow ruffled sleeves that are reminiscent of arm floats.

The jewelry and sandy blond wig is a tangled mess.

I pull down the zipper pushing one leg in and then the other.

Sassy can't hurt me.

There are things worse than her out here in the sticks.

The cotton polyester is soft against my butt and back.

I hook the yellow ruffled arm floats over round shoulders,

Laughing at the look of this dress on me.

A veil of silk shades patches of chest hair.

I gently place the ratty wig on my head,

Adjusting it accordingly over my ears.

I finger -comb it out a bit. Yeah, that's it.

All I need now are the heels

I saw her carrying in her hand

As she stumbled toward the door of the trailer

She shares with her mother and brothers

Who don't approve of her kind of entertainment.

I pull out my phone to take a few shots,

Posing in poses to post on Facebook

And tag to mutual friends

Where Sassy will surely see them

Once the hangover has worn off.

Grilled Cheese & Steak Burrito

Now I don't want it after it's been eaten.

Chewed and chewed and then swallowed.

Now I want to shove these two fingers

Down my gullet and regurgitate

It back into the metallic wrapping,

The dingy, brown bag.

A pound added is a pound

That will take me two hours

To burn on some elliptical machine.

Thighs rub together,

Arms wider than my own hands,

Swollen legs and puffy thickish feet.

Cholesterol up some more,

Blood pressure up some more.

Watch that systolic number.

If only I could tuck in this double chin

Like my godly belly.

Thinking of signing up for a *Noom* membership

Or drive to Mexico for gastric bypass surgery

Like my cousin Jackie did.

.

Pee-Wee's Pacemaker

I think of how easy it would be to run him over,

To crush every bone in that scrawny, malnourished junky body.

Feel the weight crush his skull.

There's nothing but old newspapers and bubble wrap

In that head anyway.

The only time anyone sees that sister of his is when she

Comes to collect his sorry ass for his disability check.

Everyone knows he's just going to smoke it up,

Be shit out of luck

Until the next first of the month.

I don't know what twists my tit the most: the fact he gets to take another

breath,

Or that my father talks to him more than he talks to me.

He lets him do odd and end jobs around the house

And in turn, my father acts as Pee-Wees on private ATM machine.

If I had a gun,

I would give a considerable amount of thought

In shooting him in the head execution style.

No one would blame me.

I doubt he would be missed.

Who would miss a crack-head?

I almost got my wish last week one night

When I heard the faint sound of screaming

Past my bedroom walls.

Didn't think much of it until I heard it again over my TV.

I rushed out thinking my father had collapsed in the bathroom again.

I heard the scream and then a loud wrap at the door.

It was Pee-Wee.

I had forgotten that junkies never sleep.

This pacemaker feels like somebody's kicking me in my chest,

He said in short bursts of breath.

I had no empathy to give. Fresh out.

My father left his phone in his room

So he asked me to call 9 -1-1-.

The dispatcher couldn't find us until I told her

The paramedics had been here before

To pick my dad up out of his own blood and shit.

Once she starts in with the twenty questions

About pee wee,

I handed my father the phone.

When she asked his age, and he said 64,

You could have knocked me over with a dust bunny.

More like 2004.

He screamed again to the kick of the pacemaker.

I could see red balls of light though the veil of pine trees.

He screamed again as he made his way out of my parent's driveway,

Along the dirt road where he met them

Under the streetlight in front of the house he was squatting in.

I think of how easy it could be to run him over,

To shoot him down like a rapid dog

And bury him in the backyard.

No one would miss him.

No one would care.

Turbulent

So I'm at the gym burning calories,

Trying to get this belly down,

Struggling to keep these thighs

Of mine from rubbing together

When a scenario begins to play out in my head.

The minute I enter my old room

Something feels off and unaligned.

I check around: books, art shit, bed unmade,

Rocking chair holding my backpack.

Even the glass of zero sugar cranberry juice I forgot.

Was still on the nightstand behind the industrial table fan next to the

lotion.

Something still didn't sit well until I came around the left side of the bed

By the scanner I haven't had time to hook up yet

To find that my keepsake box was missing.

Last I looked it was where it always is.

Sitting at the feet of the bed.

Inside it holds letters from poet friends,

Collage postcards,

Acceptance and rejection letters,

Gay porn DVDs,

A purple dildo I stole from a drag queen, and more.

There wasn't a place I didn't search.

Under my bed in an old entertainment center.

I turned the garage inside out from top to bottom,

Left and right looking for those things that were sitting next to my heart,

That was in racing in a state of panic.

My head was hot,

My nerves shot.

I knew I should have kept them in a place safer than this house of horrors.

I didn't bother to ask my father.

He doesn't tread on me.

He's in the face of pee wee the crack head neighbor more.

It's then that I think of my mother.

Who knows what she does in here when I'm away,

The things turned and uprooted?

I'm a tropical storm moving quickly toward her room.

She's lying in bed under a comforter too warm for the summer.

The A/C was running and every light in the room

Was too bright even for the blind.

A yellow bag from Dollar General

Was filled with *Skittles, Almond Joys*

And that nasty orange circus candy she likes to eat.

She's got dentures so she can get away with it.

Her phone is pressed on the left side of her face.

Talking to my bougie sister probably.

Have you seen that box I had sitting

At the foot of the bed?

Hold on, Erica, she tells my sister.

A what? She asked.

The box on the floor next to the nightstand my CPAP machine sits on, I told her.

I threw that mess in the garbage. I don't want that filth in my house.

Suddenly I became a category 5 hurricane shaking the house loose.

All light turned dark.

You didn't have any business touching something of mine you didn't pay for.

My mother fussed and screamed.

Is that you? Stop doing that.

All my secrets and dreams were in those letters.

I push and punch through,

Until the house is deemed a disaster area,

Displacing my parents.

I find the letters, the poems and post cards

Amongst the rubble of wood, steel and furniture.

I look up smiling in a sky standing still.

Haiku

Holes full of water

It storms outside my window

We have no power

Fast Food for the Birds

I couldn't finish the ham, egg and cheese sandwich

Cooked for breakfast this morning.

My blood pressure is sky rocketing,

Cholesterol thickening.

And I'm still trying to shake off this cough

That won't break.

Woke up Tuesday morning without taste and smell.

Left the house with Prednisone,

Benzos and Amlodipine on my stomach.

I scour the streets until I settle

On a Whataburger in midtown,

The one across the street from that new taco place.

I get a box filled with chicken tenders and

Shoestring French fries that are too salty for my heart

I barely eat anything picking over my lunch so

I feed my food to the crows, seagulls, and mottled ducks.

I leave the Texas toast. Carbs turn into sugar in the body.

A bird dips its beak in the cream gravy

As if it's some kind of mating call.

Let's hope I won't come out to find globs of seagull shit

On my car. I just got it washed on Saturday

Hungry Eyes

All I want to do is stuff him in a washing machine and douse him with Downy,

Kill the lice in his hair with what I have left of my Selsun Blue.

Scrape the Earth's filth from under those nails

Before I clip them down to the pulp.

He looks like something someone shit out

In a Dollar General dumpster.

The way he holds those pants up,

They look two sizes too small

As if he used to have the body fat to fill them out.

I gave him two bucks from my cup holder the last time.

Enough for a value meal burger,

Or a honey bun from the corner Shell.

You got any reefer? He asked.

I thought of my strawberry weed gummies

In the glove box, but didn't think that's what he had in mind.

I've been going several rounds with a cold,

So I'm glad I can't smell him.

He must have a family someplace,

A mother he keeps up nights with worry.

If these capitalists dick lickers

Are going to let him sit in the cafe

They could at least feed the poor man.

A turkey sandwich,

Birthday cake popcorn,

One of those spinach quiches.

They're just going to throw out that slice of chocolate cheesecake anyway.

 I know what it's like to go hungry,

To eat spaghetti out of a trashcan.

If it were me, I would go for broke,

Rid them of their pizza pretzels,

Jumbo peanut butter cookies,

Stuff my pockets with all the lemon squares they could hold.

I would be long gone before they could ever put their finger

On the buttons of 9-1-1.

GRENADE

GRENADE IN HAMPER OF DIRTY SHIRTS AND UNDERWEAR

GRENADE IN ROOSTER COOKIE JAR

GRANADE IN KITCHEN SINK OF SOILED SANDWICH PLATES,

   AND ORANGE JUICE GLASSES

GRENADE IN BROOM CLOSET

GRENADE IN TOASTER OVEN OF BURNT ON CHEESE

GRENADE IN BROKEN ICE MAKER

GRENADE IN VEGETABLE CRISPER

GRENADE IN LAST DRAWER ON THE LEFT OF RECIPES, LETTERS,

   AND OBITURIES.

GRENADE IN MEDICINE CABINET OF PAINKILLERS, ATHLETES
FOOT

     SPRAY BAND AIDS CINNAMON FLAVORED FLOSS

GRENADE IN WASHING MACHINE

GRENADE IN DRYER

GRENADE IN GREEN HOUSE

GRENADE IN UTILITY BUILDING

GRENADE IN NAIL GUN

GRENADE IN CAMPER

GRENADE IN SISTER'S MAKE-UP CASE

GRENADE IN LINCOLN CONTINENTAL

GRENADE IN MICROWAVE

GRENADE IN KEROSENE HEATER

GRENADE IN SECOND HAND BABY SEAT

GRENADE IN SOFA CUSHIONS

GRENADE IN STOVE

GRENADE IN RECLINER

GRENADE IN COWBOY BOOTS

GRENADE UNDER BATH TUB

GRANADE IN ATTIC

GRENADE IN BASEMENT

GRENADE STRAPED TO WATER HEATER

GRENADE TAPED TO GARAGE DOOR

GRENADE IN AIR DUCTS

GRENADE IN BLACK MAIL BOX

GRENADE IN COAT POCKET

GRENADE IN PANT POCKET

GRENADE IN SHIRT POCKET

GRENADE IN JEAN POCKET

GRENADE IN WIG

GRENADE UNDER THE BED

GRENADE IN SCHOOL

GRENADE IN CHURCH

GRENADE ON BRIDGE

GRENADE ON THE MOON WATCH IT GO BOOM

Rage

My rage will run wild

When I plunge the knife in your stomach

In the late hours of the night.

The belly that carried me.

The knife you slice ham with for Thanksgiving.

A bed full of junk food,

Ice melting in a glass of diet Coke.

The look of shock on your aging face.

The tears in your cataract eyes. You will be surprised.

This is the only way out from under you.

Blood slips from your mouth

As death rolls over you.

Your husband, my father will be next.

I'm going to bash his head in like a watermelon,

So you'll get off easy.

His hot blood spattering my face,

Staining my hands.

It's the least he could give me.

And then I'll douse the house with kerosene

Left over from winter.

My sister, your daughter, will be the only survivor

Knowing you both had it coming.

The Old Woman

Every day she comes here

With her big red bag of things she's gathered from home.

A smaller white bag,

A library book and a mug to pour the coffee

She purchased from the cafe that's not a Starbucks.

She wears that same purple sweater,

Skin tone compression socks in gray New Balances.

I assume it's butter she's smearing on a scone,

But it's sour cream on a bagel.

She opens the book from where she last left off

Only reading a few sentences at a time

Before a gentle sip from the smuggled in mug.

She can't concentrate from watching and staring.

Her purse is placed in her lap,

Positioned in a way where it can't be easily taken.

She's probably on a fixed income.

Where are her children?

Is she tethered to a husband?

She has a sweetness in her face.

She is everyone's mother.

Kids

In my dream we are two best friends

Lying on our bellies reading comic books

Strewn across your bedroom floor.

The sugar rush we're getting from the wad

Of Big League gum we're chewing is assurance

That we'll be up all night reading *The Fantastic Four*,

Captain America, *Superman* back when they were seventy five cents.

We hang loose at your parent's house

Because my mother is afraid we'll break something,

That we'll track in dirt from playing outside.

She offers us Cheetos and Capri Suns to stay away.

Our friendship is impenetrable like a GI Joe tank.

Nothing can break us after the pinky swears

And blood oaths we take using the pocket knife

Stolen from my dad's glove box.

We go around collecting worms in jelly jars,

Burning ants under magnifying glass.

When the black neighborhood kids ask,

Why are you always hanging out with that white boy?

I tell them to shut up and hold them in headlocks

Until they say sorry.

I am the biggest kid in school like The Thing from *The Fantastic Four*.

Mother would never let him in the house.

I had this dream where we were kids with superpowers,

Who could fly over buildings,

Shoot red beams out of our eyes and bend

Crowbars like licorice ropes.

I wish I had grown up with you

In Tallahassee or Kettering.

I could have used a friend like you.

Haiku

Catfish and hot grits

Salvation Army rescue

My niece is asleep

Medicine Cabinet

Opened the medicine cabinet

And out came ear drops.

The ear infection stopped

Then out came cold and flu tablets.

The tablets were expired

Then out came shoe polish.

After buffing my shoes to a high shine,

Out came hair gel.

Rubbed the gel thoroughly through

And out came deodorant.

Rolled the deodorant beneath hairless armpits

And out came athlete's foot powder.

Sprinkled the powder between my itchy toes

And out came medicated body lotion.

Massaged the lotion within the roughest, toughest

Parts of my body and out came arthritis pain pills

A little too young for pills of this sort,

So out came cologne.

Splashed its sent on a shaven face,

Then out came toothpaste.

Brushed until my gums bled

Then out came alcohol.

Poured alcohol on the wounds made after self-mutilation,

Then out came lip balm.

Smeared the lip balm across fat, cracked lips

Then out came iron supplements.

Took the iron supplements

Because the doctor said you're a little anemic,

Then out came nasal decongestant.

Cleared up my sinuses, then out came

A nail clipper. Clipped my toenails

Over a toilet bowl of blue water, then out came anti-itch cream.

Rubbed the itch cream on all that itched,

Then out came soap.

Washed all of my 2000 parts

Then that was that

Before Bed

Take the plate into the kitchen,

Put the cup in the freezer,

The chicken in the fridge,

Get my socks off the counter,

Gather the flashcards into a rubber band tightly.

I like things in their place, filed away, sorted & neat.

Tuck the notes from a working novel

Into my journal,

Switch off the TV.

I've seen this episode.

Tired of being tired.

Hate getting old.

The chicken will sit in my belly,

Keep in my colon until morning.

Floss more, brush teeth.

Scott, Richard's friend, has big blue eyes

& Yellow teeth from the cigarettes.

Can tell he used to be pretty once.

Think of his dick in jeans bluer than his eyes. This before bed.

Shower the filth of the day off me into the drain,

Stare at myself in the mirror,

Reflections of belly & man-tits.

Unplug the charger,

Grab the book,

Grab my wallet & phone,

Switch off the lights,

The fan.

Sit the notebook anywhere,

Place my phone on a portfolio of collages,

Drawings, and naked men cut out of magazines.

Slip myself into bed.

Fuck getting old as long as I can still get hard-ons.

Poet, Novelist, Anthologist, Pervert, Homosexualist, Collagist, and Blogger, SHANE ALLISON is the author of the novels *You're The One I Want* and *Harm Done* (Strebor Books). He is also the author of *Slut Machine* (Queer Mojo Press) and *I remember* (Future Tense Book). He lives in Tallahassee.

HYSTERICAL BOOKS
TALLAHASSEE, FL 2024